I Want You to Know

Mona Damluji

Ishtar Bäcklund Dakhil

SEVEN STORIES PRESS
New York ★ Oakland ★ London

*For Layaal and Zayn, and our ancestors,
whose stories we carry in our hearts.*
—M.D.

*To all my ancestors who have come before,
to my family whom I love beyond words, and to all
our beloveds who are coming; the love we share
heals through time and space.*
—I.B.D.

I want you to know
that you come from a place
and a people that are beautiful.

I want you to know
that our ancestors loved
and laughed and danced
and played and worked
and cared for one another
in this place.

They called this place home.

I want you to know
that they were not perfect,
your ancestors,
because no one is.

Yet they lived in dignity.

And I want you to know
that what made this place unsafe was greed.
The greed of people from another place
who already have more than they need.

Those people who have so much,
and still want more,
they made war.

They made horrible, ugly, impossible war.

The war took away buildings,
took away homes,
made it unsafe to stay,
made so many leave.

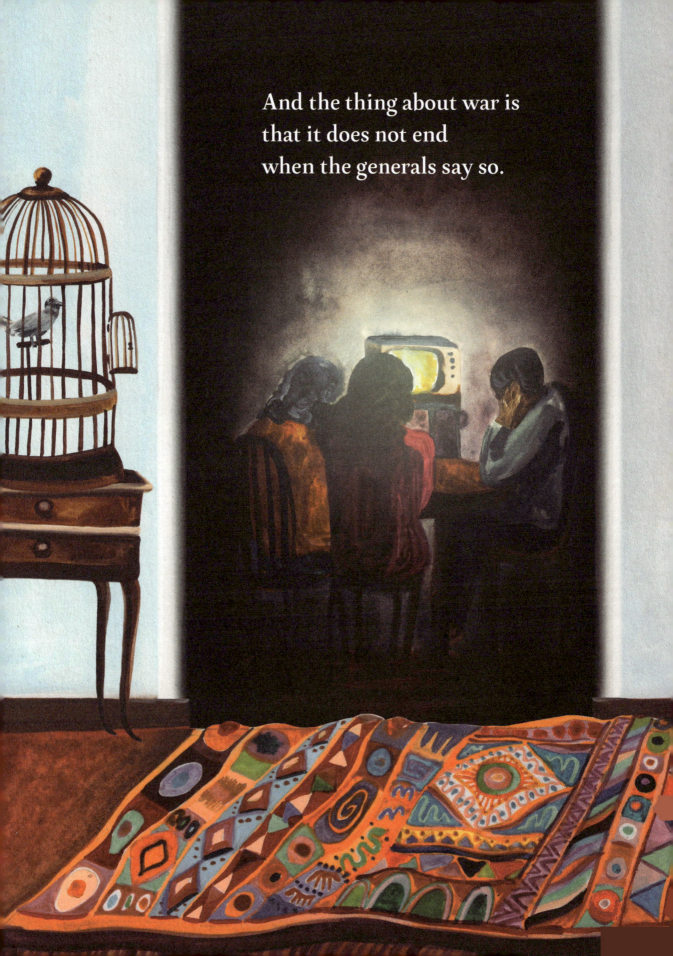

It burns in the heart,
and in the minds,
and into the pockets.

War keeps burning
in those who witness,
in those displaced,
and all those who remember.

It burns in our questions,
and burns in our pain.

War set ablaze the street
our ancestors called home.
It turned off the lights,
made day into night.

And so they left,
like those who left before.

I want you to know
you do not carry it all alone.

And from this fire,
something beautiful can grow.

However far away we are now,
however many miles,
however many years,

I want you to know
that you are still of the place
our ancestors have known.

The place that they called home.

A TRIANGLE SQUARE BOOK FOR YOUNG READERS
published by
SEVEN STORIES PRESS

Copyright © 2025 by Mona Damluji and Ishtar Bäcklund Dakhil

All rights reserved.
No part of this book may be reproduced,
stored in a retrieval system, or transmitted in any form or by
any means, including mechanical, electronic, photocopying, recording,
or otherwise, without the prior written permission of the publisher.

SEVEN STORIES PRESS
140 Watts Street
New York, NY 10013
www.sevenstories.com

Teachers may order free examination copies of Seven Stories Press titles.
Visit https://www.sevenstories.com/pg/resources-academics
or email academic@sevenstories.com.

LIBRARY OF CONGRESS CATALOGING-IN-PUBLICATION DATA IS ON FILE

ISBN: 978-1-64421-441-1 (hardcover)
ISBN: 978-1-64421-442-8 (ebook)

PRINTED IN CANADA

9 8 7 6 5 4 3 2 1

MONA DAMLUJI grew up on the other side of the world from the places that her ancestors called home. Yet, thanks to her parents and grandparents, she has always felt a deep attachment to her Iraqi and Lebanese roots. As a student, Mona moved around quite a bit, calling many places home from Beirut to Boston, Berkeley, London, and China. Today she lives in Santa Barbara, California where she works as a college professor in Film and Media Studies. When Mona is not hanging out with her kids, she's likely teaching, writing, organizing poetry readings, or dreaming up creative projects.

ISHTAR BÄCKLUND DAKHIL was born in Sweden to Iraqi and Finnish parents. She's been painting her whole life and completed her BA in illustration and MFA in visual communication at Konstfack University of Arts, Crafts and Design in Stockholm and the California College of the Arts in San Francisco. Recently, she has been working with children and communities around the world, from Guadalajara, Mexico, to the Hawaiian Islands, creating community-based art projects and pursuing her passion for picture-book making. When she's not drawing and painting, you can find Ishtar in the surf somewhere catching waves!